IT'S OKAY TO MAKE MISTAKES

UH-OH

TODD PARR

Megan Tingley Books

LITTLE, BROWN AND COMPANY

NEW YORK BOSTON

Also by Todd Parr

Love the World
The Goodbye Book
Otto Goes to School
Otto Goes to the Beach
The Underwear Book
The I'm Not Scared Book
The Peace Book
Reading Makes You Feel Good
We Belong Together
The Thankful Book

The Mommy Book
The Daddy Book
The Grandma Book
The Grandpa Book
The Family Book
It's Okay to Be Different
The Feelings Book
The Feel Good Book
The Earth Book
The I Love You Book

A complete list of Todd's books and more
information can be found at toddparr.com.

About This Book

The art for this book was created on a drawing tablet using an iMac, starting with bold black lines and dropping in color with Adobe Photoshop. Lots of mistakes were made when creating this book—they helped make the final product great!

Love, Todd

This book was edited by Liza Baker and designed by Saho Fujii. The text was set in Todd Parr's signature font. The production was supervised by Erika Schwartz, and the production editor was Wendy Dopkin.

To Morgan, Dominic, Spencer, Gibson, Sam, Addi,
Cadince, Nora, Georgianna, and Paige

Love, "Uncle" Todd

It's okay if you spill your milk.

You can always clean it up.

It's okay to try a different direction.

You might discover something new.

It's okay to not know the answer.

Asking questions helps you learn.

It's okay to get upset.

Your friends are there to cheer you on.

It's okay to fall down.

You can always get back up.

It's okay to wear two different socks.

UH-OH

Others may try it, too.

It's okay to forget your umbrella.

You might meet someone new.

It's okay to change your mind.

Everyone is ready at a different time.

It's okay to get mixed up.

You can always ask for help.

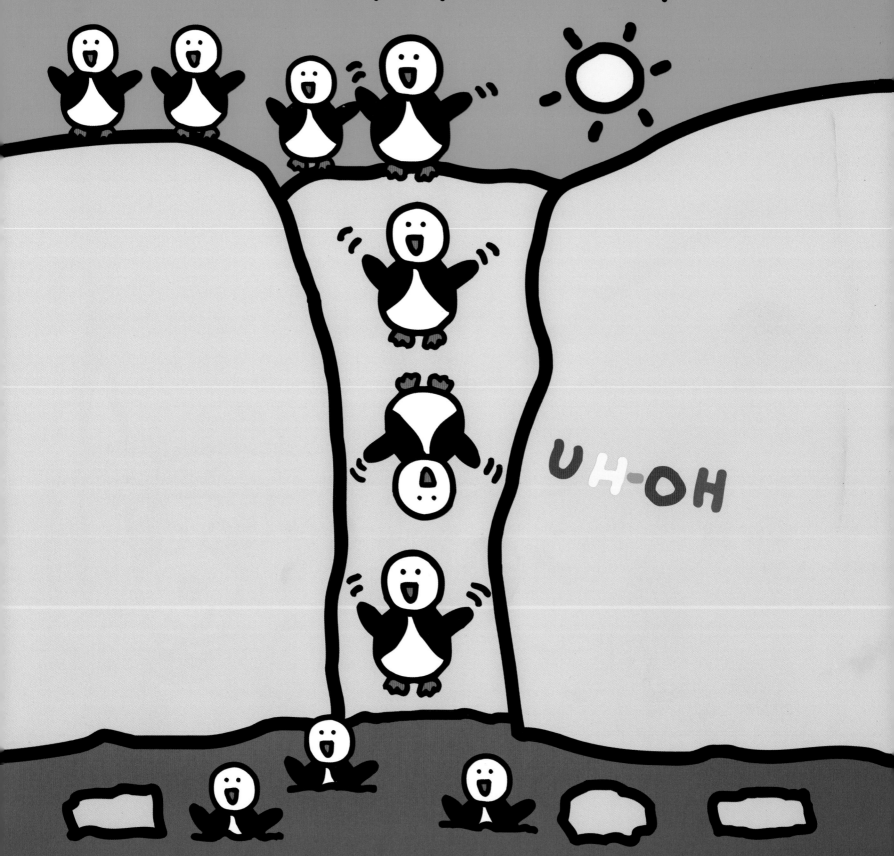

You might invent a new move.

It's okay to get dirty.

UH-OH

A bubble bath is lots of fun.

Being quiet can make you a good listener.

It's okay to color outside the lines.

It's good to follow your own path.

Everyone has "uh-oh" moments.

It's okay to make mistakes sometimes. Everyone does – even grown-ups! That's how we learn.

The End.

Love, Todd